CHICAGO

CUBS

NL
EAST

MICHAEL E. GOODMAN

Published by Creative Education, Inc.

123 S. Broad Street, Mankato, Minnesota 56001

Art Director, Rita Marshall
Cover and title page design by Virginia Evans
Cover and title page illustration by Rob Day
Type set by FinalCopy Electronic Publishing
Book design by Rita Marshall

Photos by Allsport, Mel Bailey, Duomo,
Focus on Sports, Diane Johnson, Sportschrome,
UPI/Bettmann and Wide World Photos

**Library of Congress Cataloging-in-Publication Data**

Goodman, Michael E.

Chicago Cubs / by Michael E. Goodman.

p.   cm.

Summary: A team history of the Chicago Cubs,
featuring outstanding players over the years.

ISBN 0-88682-464-8

1. Chicago Cubs (Baseball team)—History—
Juvenile literature.   [1. Chicago Cubs (Baseball
team)—History.   2. Baseball—History.]   I. Title.

GV875.C6G67 1991                          91-10381

796.357'64'0977311—dc20                         CIP

## THE HOME OF THE CUBS

Centuries ago, Indians living along the southern shore of Lake Michigan noticed a strong smell of wild onions carried by powerful winds that blew in the area. The word in their language that described the smell was "Checagou," and that is what they named the place. In time, the people who settled in the area changed the spelling to "Chicago."

The wild onions were replaced long ago by tall buildings, paved streets, and the bustle of traffic. But the strong winds have remained, and they are responsible for Chicago's most famous nickname, the "Windy City."

One of the places the winds are felt most strongly is Wrigley Field, where the Chicago Cubs of the National League play their home games. Those winds have helped

*A Chicago superstar, Billy Williams.*

**1 8 7 6**

*William A. Hulbert became president of the new NL, a position he held until his death in 1882.*

carry balls hit by Cub stars over Wrigley's ivy-covered walls since the 1920s. Among those Chicago sluggers have been Hack Wilson, Gabby Hartnett, Ernie Banks, Billy Williams, Ron Santo, Dave Kingman, Andre Dawson, and Ryne Sandberg.

Windy Wrigley Field is one of the smallest major-league baseball stadiums in numbers of seats, but not in the amount of noise generated by its patrons. No fans are louder or more loyal than those of the Cubs. There is a special relationship between the Cubs and their followers. The love affair has been going strong since the team first joined the National League in 1876 and won the first of its ten pennants. And even though the team has not played in a World Series since 1945, the constant support of Cub fans' is well known. In fact, a play was once written about the famous "Bleacher Bums" at Wrigley Field, who come out day after day to cheer for their heroes.

One of the reasons for the close relationship between the Cubs and their fans is that the team has always cared a lot about its followers, especially the young ones. The club has given away hundreds of thousands of tickets over the years to Boy Scouts, Little Leaguers, and others, just so the kids could see their favorite team play. Also, most of the Cubs' home games are played in the afternoon, when kids can easily attend. Lights, to be used during night games, were not even installed at Wrigley Field until 1988.

From the very start, the Cubs' founders were as concerned about the team's fans as they were about the players. That concern helped get the National League—and modern-day baseball—underway.

*The Cubs and their fans—a special relationship.*

*On August 6, player/
manager Cap Anson
slammed three
homers in three
consecutive at-bats.*

**T**he Cubs' first forefather was William A. Hulbert, who owned the team, then called the "White Stockings," in the 1870s. By 1875, Hulbert was worried. Things weren't going too well. On the field, the team had a losing record. Off the field, gambling scandals and other problems were threatening to destroy professional baseball.

Hulbert decided that something had to be done to correct the problems. He went around the country and met with owners of the strongest clubs in the old National Association to convince them to form a new league. The organization—to be called the National League—would have strict rules concerning gambling and behavior of players and fans.

Before Chicago played its first game in the new league, Hulbert made sure his team had some of the top talent. He convinced several outstanding players to come to Chicago, including pitcher/manager Albert Spalding.

The White Stockings got off to a great start in the new league in 1876—mostly because of Al Spalding. As manager, Spalding led Chicago to the first National League pennant with a 52–14 record. As pitcher, the iron-armed Spalding won a remarkable forty-seven games!

A few years later, Spalding left his playing days behind to set up a sporting goods company that is still around today. He also took over as president of the Chicago club and hired a new player/manager named Adrian "Cap" Anson, who led the team as hitter and skipper to five pennants between 1880 and 1886.

"Cap Anson was a baseball pioneer," said one sportswriter. "He was one of the first to use the hit-and-run, coaching signals, a pitching rotation, and spring training. He was also a mean-spirited guy who marched his team onto the field in military formation and demanded very strict behavior. His players often hated him, but he helped them become winners."

## TURN-OF-THE-CENTURY LEGENDS

*Jack Taylor led the Cubs with 22 victories and the entire NL with a 1.33 ERA.*

**A**l Spalding and Cap Anson helped the White Stockings become a National League power in the 1800s. In 1902, a new manager named Frank Selee took over the team that had changed its nickname to "Cubs" the prior year. Selee lasted only three years as Cubs manager, but he made a major contribution to the team's history.

Selee decided to shake things up right away. He moved catcher Frank Chance to first base. Then he had Joe Tinker switch from third base to shortstop. Next, he brought up a young shortstop named Johnny Evers and put him at second base between Tinker and Chance. All of these changes of position could have confused the players, but the three men worked very well together. They turned many a ball hit to short into an easy double play. One New York sportswriter and Giants fan named Franklin P. Adams got so annoyed at seeing the Cub trio double up Giant runners that he wrote a poem that began: "These are the saddest of possible words/Tinker-to-Evers-to-Chance." Soon baseball fans all over America began to recite the poem. It made the Cubs infielders famous and may even have helped them get elected together to the Hall of Fame.

*Former Cub reliever Mitch Williams.*

*A legend-in-the-making, Jerome Walton.*

*Proving he was not only a fine manager, Frank Chance (right) tied for the team home run lead—with 2!*

Selee, before he left the team because of illness in 1905 and turned over the manager's reins to Frank Chance, also brought in two outstanding pitchers. They were Mordecai "Three-Fingered" Brown (he had lost part of two fingers in an accident as a child) and Ed Reulbach. Between 1906 and 1908, this pair of hurlers achieved the almost impossible: They compiled a combined record of 135 wins and only 36 losses as the Cubs won three National League pennants.

Chicago won the first two of those pennants the normal way—they outhit and outpitched their league opponents. But in 1908, they won the pennant by outthinking their chief rival, the New York Giants.

The Giants and Cubs were playing a crucial series in New York in late September of 1908. The Cubs took the first two games, and the third was tied in the bottom of the ninth, with Giant runners Moose McCormick on third and Fred Merkle on first. The next batter smashed a single to center field. Giants fans began to pour onto the field as McCormick crossed the plate. Merkle, seeing the crowd, decided to head to the locker room without touching second base. Lots of runners did that in those days, even though the rules say that, to complete the play, Merkle had to step on second or he could be forced out and the run wouldn't count.

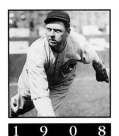

1 9 0 8

*Three-Fingered Brown established a club record by winning 29 games, a mark that still stands.*

"Everyone thought the game was over," recalled Giant player Fred Snodgrass. "Everyone except Johnny Evers, anyway. Evers began calling for the ball. He made so much noise about getting the ball and stepping on second that he got the umpires' attention, and they were already heading to the clubhouse.

"Finally Hank O'Day, the senior umpire, ruled that Merkle was indeed out, and our run didn't count," Snodgrass continued. "The game ended in a tie. We ended the season tied for first place with the Cubs, and the game had to be played over to decide the pennant. As you know, the Cubs beat us in that playoff game, so we didn't win the pennant. We thought the call on Merkle was a raw deal, but what could we do?"

Merkle's mistake helped the Cubs win their third straight National League pennant. Chicago went on to capture its second consecutive World Series as well, as the Cubs outhit and outpitched Ty Cobb's Detroit Tigers four games to one. Cubs teams have won several other National League pennants since 1908, but sadly, that was the last time Cubs fans have been able to root for a world champion.

## "GABBY" AND "HACK" LEAD A CUB REVIVAL

1 9 1 6

*The Cubs moved into Weeghman Park, which today is known as Wrigley Field.*

**T**he Cubs were up and down over the next twenty years. They topped the National League again in 1910 and 1918, but then began to sink in the standings. They finally hit rock bottom in 1925.

But things were soon going to improve. In the mid-1920s, two new stars arrived in the Windy City. They went by the strange nicknames of "Gabby" and "Hack."

Charles Leo Hartnett was one of the finest defensive catchers in baseball for twenty seasons, and was also an excellent hitter. Hartnett did one other thing very well— he loved to talk to opposing batters and distract them at the plate. So sportswriters began calling him "Gabby" Hartnett, and the nickname stuck.

Gabby might have annoyed opponents with his chatter, but his teammates loved him. Charley Root, who pitched to Hartnett for sixteen years in Chicago, said, "He got the best out of you. If you were letting down, Gabby would fire the ball back at you like a shot. Believe me, that woke you up on the mound. My own experience with him catching was that he always called the right pitch. He was daring at all times, and sure of himself. He made a pitcher feel that way, too."

In 1926, Gabby was joined on the Cubs by Lewis Wilson, a short, powerful slugger. Wilson looked like a famous wrestler of the time named George Hackenschmidt, so teammates began calling him "Hack." He could certainly hack at pitches thrown to him, sending screaming line drives regularly over the fences at Wrigley Field. During one season (1930), he set two records that still stand. He slugged fifty-six home runs—

14       *Like Wilson, Andre Dawson is a powerful slugger.*

*For the fourth
consecutive season
Cub slugger Hack
Wilson (right) led
the National League
in homers.*

the most ever in National League history—and drove in
an unbelievable 190 runs, a total that has never been
topped in either league.

Gabby and Hack led the Cubs back to the top of the
National League in 1929, but the team lost in the World
Series to Connie Mack's Philadelphia Athletics. The Cubs
captured pennants in 1932 and 1935 as well, but still won
no championships. Every three years, Chicago seemed
to come out on top. So, as the 1938 season came around,
Cubs fans figured they were in for an exciting year. They
were right!

The pennant race went down to the wire, with the
Pittsburgh Pirates leading the Cubs by a half-game with
just a few games remaining in the season. The two teams
faced off in a titanic struggle in Chicago. The score was
tied 5–5 going into the ninth. It was getting pretty dark,

and there were no lights in Wrigley Field, of course. The umpires said the game would be called and would have to be replayed if neither team scored in the ninth inning.

The Pirates went down in order in their half of the inning, and the first two Cubs also made outs. Then Gabby Hartnett stepped to the plate. He was doing double duty that year as Cub catcher and manager. Gabby, who was having trouble seeing the ball, took two quick strikes from Pirate ace reliever Mace Brown. The next pitch came whizzing toward the plate, and Gabby swung where he thought the ball must be. He connected, and the ball went sailing toward the left-field stands. The players never actually saw it go over the fence, but the fans in left certainly did. They let out a roar. Gabby Hartnett's famous shot, known as "the homer in the gloaming (darkness)," helped make the Cubs National League champs once again!

Reflecting on the event years later, Pirate star Paul Waner remembered, "I just stood there in right field and watched Hartnett circle the bases, and take the lousy pennant with him. I just watched and wondered. I've never seen anything like it before or since."

*Gabby Hartnett was named to the NL All-Star squad for the sixth consecutive season.*

---

## "MR. CUB"

The Cubs captured one final National League pennant in 1945 and then began a steady decline for the next twenty years. Some great players starred in Chicago during the 1950s and 1960s, but they never got to wear a championship ring. Among these "ringless" stars were iron man Billy Williams, who once played in

*The celebrated career of Mr. Cub, Ernie Banks (right), began in Chicago.*

more than eleven hundred consecutive games and was one of baseball's top outfielders; power-hitting third baseman Ron Santo; smooth-fielding shortstop Don Kessinger; and pitching stars Moe Drabowsky, Ken Holtzman, and Ferguson Jenkins.

But perhaps the Cubs player who most deserved to play on a winning team was a slender, power-hitting infielder named Ernie Banks. He was so good for so many years that he earned the nickname "Mr. Cub" from his adoring fans in Chicago.

Banks didn't look like a slugger: he was 6'1" and weighed only 180 pounds. But he had powerful wrists and arms. "You grab hold of him," said Cub manager Bob Scheffing, "and it's like grabbing hold of steel."

Banks also had a great attitude, even when his team was losing. The Cubs might be hopelessly out of a pennant race, but Banks would still tell his teammates, "We're going to win today. You watch. The Cubbies are making their move." He helped everyone enjoy playing just a little bit more.

Every year, Chicago fans could count on "Mr. Cub." Five times, he slugged forty or more home runs in a season. No shortstop in baseball history had ever had that kind of power. The Cubs finished in sixth place in two of those years, 1958 and 1959, but sportswriters recognized Banks's greatness. They elected him the league's Most Valuable Player both seasons.

In 1969, Cubs fans also took a vote, and Banks was easily elected "the greatest Cub of all time." After he retired in 1972, Banks was a shoo-in for the Hall of Fame, and sure enough, was elected to the Hall the first year he was eligible.

*Don Cardwell became the only pitcher in history to hurl a no-hitter in his first appearance for a club.*

## NEAR MISSES AND A BULLS-EYE

Ernie Banks almost got to play on a championship Cubs team in 1969. That year, Chicago jumped out to an early lead in the National League East Division and was up by nine and a half games over the New York Mets in mid-August. Banks, Ron Santo, and Billy Williams all hit more than twenty home runs that season, and Ferguson Jenkins won twenty-one games. But the Cubs faded in late August, losing eight in a row while the Mets won ten straight.

Santo, Williams, and Jenkins were also around in 1973, when Chicago broke out to another early lead. Once again, however, the Mets caught them, and the Cubs faded out of sight.

*Another Cub standout, pitcher Rick Sutcliffe.*

Cubs players and fans were disappointed, but they remembered the words that Ernie Banks had spoken just before he retired in 1972: "Never give up. No matter what, a Cub never quits. Never. Never."

It would take eleven more years, but in 1984, "Mr. Cub's" optimism finally paid off. The Cubs broke out quickly, and at the end of April were tied for first place with the Mets. This time, unlike in 1969 and 1973, the Cubs left the Mets behind. Chicago continued to rise in the standings. Then the team made a key trade for pitcher Rick Sutcliffe at mid-season. The big right-hander compiled a remarkable 16–1 record for Chicago in only half a year, and helped keep the Cubs competitive in the race for the East Division crown.

1 9 7 9

*Relief pitcher Bruce Sutter capped a fantastic season by winning the NL Cy Young award.*

"I felt very good about the way in which our ball club went out on the field and played from April through October," manager Jim Frey said. "I never got the feeling a player wasn't giving 100 percent."

Frey was proudest of his second baseman on the 1984 team, twenty-three-year-old Ryne Sandberg. If the trade for Sutcliffe was a key to the Cubs' success in 1984, the swap made two years before with the Philadelphia Phillies that brought Sandberg to the Windy City was even more important to the team's future.

Amazingly, Sandberg was just a throw-in in the 1982 trade with Philadelphia. The key players in the deal were shortstops Ivan DeJesus and Larry Bowa. The Cubs felt they were giving up more by trading DeJesus to the Phillies and demanded another player, Sandberg.

Frey made Sandberg his third baseman in 1982, and then switched him to second a year later. He has been starring there ever since.

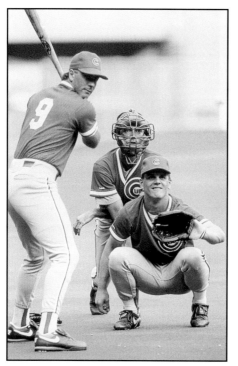

*Left to right: Damon Berryhill, Lee Smith, Dick Bordi, Ferguson Jenkins.*

Before the 1984 season began, Frey took Sandberg aside. "You see yourself as a singles hitter," the manager said, "but I think you have the speed and power to hit thirty-five to forty doubles a year, eight to ten triples, and, in time, lots of home runs. You look like you're just trying to meet the ball, and I think you can drive the ball."

That advice changed Sandberg's career forever—and changed the Cubs' fortunes for the better, too. Driving the ball in 1984, Sandberg hit thirty-six doubles, nineteen triples, and nineteen home runs. He batted .314 and won the Gold Glove as the best fielding second baseman in the National League. He was also named the league's Most Valuable Player. He has gotten even better since 1984. By 1990, he had become one of the league's leading home-run hitters and RBI men. To prove he was a complete player, Sandberg also set a major-league record in 1990 for most consecutive games without an error at second base.

*Ryne Sandberg established a NL record for fielding percentage by a second baseman with a .9938 mark.*

"Ryne Sandberg is the best second baseman I've ever played with," said Larry Bowa, an all-star himself for many seasons. "He does everything so effortlessly—goes after and catches almost every ball and has a great arm. Plus he has an outstanding bat. He's simply a natural."

Sandberg's natural talent helped the Cubs win their first title of any kind since 1945—the 1984 National League East Division crown. After several near misses, the Cubs had finally hit a bull's-eye. There was joy in Chicago once again.

*The unbelievable Ryne Sandberg (page 26–27).*

## THE HAWK AND THE KIDS

*On August 13, the Cubs retired Hall-of-Famer Billy Williams's jersey, number 26.*

**T**he Cubs' joy was short-lived, however. Chicago lost to the San Diego Padres in a tight playoff series for the 1984 National League pennant. A Chicago sportswriter noted, "Cubs players and fans alike were crushed, dumbfounded. What had seemed all but theirs—the club's first National League pennant since 1945—suddenly slipped through their grasp." Cubs management, as a result, began looking for additional stars to back up Sandberg and Sutcliffe.

The first priority was a power hitter. The perfect choice was unhappily laboring north of the border in Montreal. Andre Dawson, whose nickname was "The Hawk," had been starring for ten seasons with the Montreal Expos, but he was ready to move on. Dawson wanted more money, a natural grass field to protect his fragile knees, and lots of wind to carry his line shots over the outfield fences. The Cubs and Wrigley Field fulfilled all of his requirements. He signed on with Chicago as a free agent before the 1987 season.

In his first year in the Windy City, The Hawk slammed forty-nine homers, drove in 137 runs, and was named the National League's Most Valuable Player. But his performance was still not enough to make the Cubs into big winners.

So the team turned to its farm system and began calling up a string of hungry young players. Leading the youth movement at the plate and in the field are shortstop Shawon Dunston—whose bat was always strong, but whose fielding has been improving each year—and slick-fielding and smooth-hitting first baseman Mark Grace.

*Mike Bielecki (left) had the best season of his major league career, recording 18 victories.*

Grace can pull the ball to right field or smack it to left when he wants. "Hitting to all fields is something I take pride in," he says. "When you're one-dimensional, you're easy to defense."

Then, in 1989, Chicago called up two outstanding new rookies—Jerome Walton and Dwight Smith. These two outfielders placed first and second in the voting for National League Rookie of the Year in 1989.

On the mound, the Cubs added youngster Greg Maddux as a starter and traded for starter Mike Bielecki and relief ace Mitch Williams. "Maddux has a great curveball and change-up," says pitching coach Dick Pole, "and his fastball does something different every time." Bielecki was the team's big winner with nineteen victories in 1989, and Williams tied the club record with thirty-six saves the same season.

*Chicago ace Greg Maddux.*

*First baseman Mark Grace.*          31

**1 9 9 1**

*With the addition of key new players and a healthy Jerome Walton the Cubs were a pennant contender.*

"We're all still new to the game, still learning what it takes to win," says Maddux. "We've come up just happy to be here, but when that wears off, you start thinking about winning."

And winning is what the Cubs have been doing. The team was not expected to do very well in 1989 because it was so young. But Chicago surprised the experts by capturing another East Division title. Once again, the NL pennant eluded the Cubs' grasp, however, as the hard-hitting San Francisco Giants won the league title after a classic playoff series.

Injuries to Walton, Smith, Maddux, and Bielecki in 1990 hurt Chicago's chances to win a second straight East Division title and have another shot at the National League pennant. Still, the Cubbies won't be down for long.

"Watch out for our kids," says former Cub manager Don Zimmer. "These guys are easy to manage, they get along, and they play hard. Pretty soon, people will join our announcer Harry Caray when he yells, 'Cubs win! Cubs win! Cubs win!'"

796.357 Goodman, Michael E
GOO
       Chicago Cubs : NL
       East


                                    $12.50

| DATE DUE | BORROWER | |
|---|---|---|
| MAR 14 1995 | | |
| | | |
| | | |
| | | |
| | | |


796.357 Goodman, Michael E
GOO
       Chicago Cubs : NL
       East


                              $12.50


BLOOMER MIDDLE SCHOOL LIB
1325 15TH AVE
BLOOMER, WI 54724

 GUMDROP BOOKS - Bethany, Missouri